Y0-BWY-871

CARING FOR MY NEW KITTEN

John Bankston

Mitchell Lane
PUBLISHERS

2001 SW 31st Avenue
Hallandale, FL 33009
www.mitchelllane.com

First Edition, 2019.

Author: John Bankston
Designer: Ed Morgan
Editor: Sharon F. Doorasamy

Names/credits:
Title: Caring for My New Kitten / by John Bankston
Description: Hallandale, FL : Mitchell Lane Publishers, [2019]

Series: How to Care for Your New Pet

Library bound ISBN: 9781680203202

eBook ISBN: 9781680203219

Photo credits: Design elements and photos, Freepik.com

CONTENTS

Words in **bold** throughout can be found in the Glossary.

A Brief History of Cats

Cats love chasing mice. Mice eat crops. This is why farmers let cats roam around their fields. Thousands of years ago, Egyptians welcomed cats into their homes. In the 1800s, people began **breeding** cats.

House cats are related to wild cats such as lions, tigers, and cougars. They are gifted **predators**. Cats are the least tamed pets. They are amazing hunters—even just hunting a toy. They are also **independent**. This means they look out for themselves. This is one reason cats are so popular.

Like people, every cat is different. Some will follow their special person. Some will greet you when you return home from school. There are almost 100 **breeds** of cats. They include the Maine Coon, the American Curl, and the Japanese Bobtail. Which one will you want?

DID YOU KNOW?

People who killed cats in ancient Egypt were killed as punishment.

Cat Facts

Cats eat meat. They have long, sharp teeth. Their tongue is rough. It feels like sandpaper. They use it to lick themselves clean. Their ears resemble triangles. Their eyes are big—the better to see you with. They use their whiskers to find their way in tight places.

Cats have **retractable** claws. This means the claws can disappear. Claws on a dog's paws do not retract. Cats have five toes on their front feet, and four on their back feet.

Maybe you'll choose a long-haired cat like a Persian. Maybe you'll bring a short-haired Siamese home. Your new kitten could become your best friend. But taking care of a kitten is hard work. There are things to do before you bring your "fur baby" home.

DID YOU KNOW?

Kittens have baby teeth. They usually lose them at around six months.

Finding the Purr-fect Pet

Millions of cats don't have homes. Your town probably has a local **shelter** or rescue center. Their websites will have pictures of cats and kittens. These pets are available for **adoption**. Shelters also list available breeds.

You can also buy a cat from a breeder. These men and women raise one or two types of cats.

Maybe you know a friend or family member whose cat just had kittens. This is a great way to adopt. If you know what mama cat is like, you will have an idea how her kittens will act. Remember, kittens need to stay with their mom until they are at least eight weeks old.

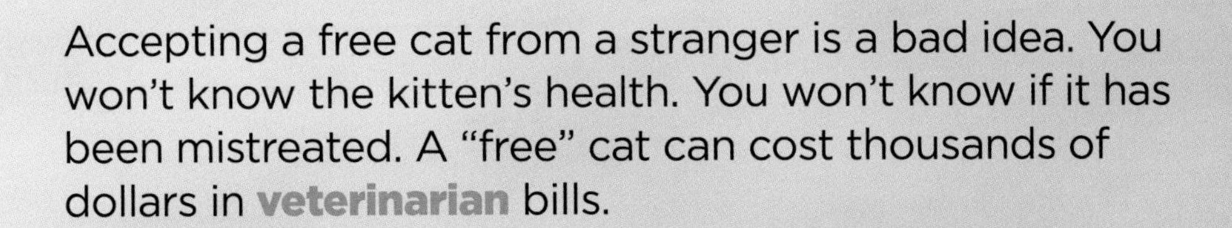

Accepting a free cat from a stranger is a bad idea. You won't know the kitten's health. You won't know if it has been mistreated. A "free" cat can cost thousands of dollars in **veterinarian** bills.

Kittens are fun, playful, and very, very cute. But like human babies they need lots of care. Caring for adult cats is usually easier. They will probably be housebroken. Most adult rescue cats are healthy and friendly. Many kitten care tips work for cats as well. You can teach an older cat new tricks.

Meeting Kitten

Your pet will soon be a part of the family. Unlike other family members, you'll get a say in whether it comes home with you.

Picking a kitten is tons of fun. Just remember, it's also picking you. Not every kitten bonds with every person. Spend time with it. Play a little. Rub its head between its ears. Does it hiss? Does it seem very tired? This may not be the right kitten for you.

Shelters usually won't let you take the kitten home right away. They will ask you to come back. This lets you think about your new friend. Are you really ready to take care of a kitten? Are you ready for the hard work, not just the fun? Kittens aren't candy bars. You need to be sure you are ready.

Getting Ready

Have you ever had a friend stay over? Did you make up a spare bed? Did you put out clean towels? Maybe you had a parent buy their favorite food. Your kitten will be in your home for years. It needs to feel welcome.

Your kitten should be kept in a small space. Even an adult cat should not be allowed to wander around the house at first. Your room or a spare bathroom is ideal. It needs to have a door you can shut. There are also pet gates you can use.

It is not a good idea to keep a kitten in a basement or a garage. There are just too many ways for them to get into trouble. Like babies, kittens put lots of gross things into their mouths. Paint, antifreeze, detergent, and house plants are all poisonous to cats.

When you have chosen the right place, clean it up. Remove your clothing and toys. Adults in your house can help. They may want to buy a cat bed or use an old blanket. Some rescue centers will give you a towel or blanket that the kitten slept on. This helps it feel less homesick.

You will also need to buy two metal bowls for food and water. Make sure they are "kitten-sized." Set the kitten's litter box away from where it sleeps and eats. A private corner is best.

DID YOU KNOW?

The cat is the only animal that purrs. No one is sure why.

Bringing Kitty Home

The day has arrived! Your new kitty is ready to come home. The shelter or breeder may provide a **carrier**. This is a way to carry your cat home.

Playing with your new friend is more than just fun. It helps the kitty become **socialized**. This is how kittens learn to get along with people and other animals. If there is a friendly dog in the house, you can introduce them. *Do not leave them alone.* Scared kittens can scratch.

Let kitty decide how much it wants to play. Sit on the floor. Let it come to you.

If you have brothers or sisters, they will want to play too. One or two at a time is best. Too many people might make it scared.

Moving to its forever home is tiring. Let it nap. You should also set your kitten down in the litter box. This is how you teach it to use it.

DID YOU KNOW?

A female cat is called a queen. A male is called a tom.

Litter Box Tips

Fill the litter box about two inches high with unscented litter. Cats have a better sense of smell than we do. They may not like the smell of scented litter.

Your kitten's new room is like its **den**. They will want to keep it neat. This is why they will use the litter box instead of your rug.

Scoop out the box every day. If you don't, they may stop using it. Once a week wash it with soap and hot water.

Keep the litter box in a private, quiet space.

Just like toddlers, kittens make mistakes. Sometimes they will go when they get scared or excited. If you see them start to go, say "No!" in a firm voice. Then carry them to the box. Be gentle and kind. You can reward them with a kitten treat. Never yell at your cat or hit it. Be sweet to it and it will be sweet to you.

DID YOU KNOW?

At Moscow Cats Theatre, cats do tricks like walking tightropes and jumping over dogs.

A Kitten's Favorite Thing

Do you know the one thing kittens do more than anything else? Sleep! A kitten grows into an adult cat in about one year. That takes a lot of energy.

Kittens sleep around 16 hours a day. That's probably six hours more than you sleep. Let them have all the peaceful naps they want. Besides, kittens are cute when they are sleeping. And when they wake up? Playtime!

DID YOU KNOW?

"Kitten season" is from May to September. This is when most cats give birth.

Playtime

What did you think about when you thought about getting a kitten? Was it playtime? Playtime with your new friend can be lots of fun. Just be careful. Kittens and cats have claws and teeth. You don't want your hand to be a chew toy. The best games let your new friend follow their **instincts**.

Cats love to hunt. Your sweet kitten will act like a crouching lion. Toss a rolled up napkin. Let the kitten chase it. Some toys are attached to string you can pull. Kittens prefer ones that look like mice. Kittens will also chase a beam of light. Some even like climbing into empty bags or boxes. They pretend it's their den.

Kittens love to play with string or yarn. They enjoy chasing ping-pong balls. Never let your kitten play with toys when you aren't watching. They can easily choke. Keep the toys in a drawer. Play with different ones so they don't get bored. As your kitten gets older, you will notice it getting better at playing. Young kittens can be clumsy!

Your kitten will soon be able to climb onto window sills. This is why you should never leave windows open in rooms they are in. They can even push out screens. If you have a backyard bird feeder, it will be like kitty TV.

Playtime is more than just fun. It helps your kitten grow into a happy cat.

Grooming

Besides getting them used to playtime, you will want them to get used to being groomed. Brushing your kitten is very important. You should do this a few times a week. It will keep their hair from getting matted. It will also reduce hairballs.

DID YOU KNOW?

The catnip that makes your cat nutty is a plant from the mint family.

Food and Water

Besides love and a litter box, you need to give your kitten the right food.

Kittens should be with their mothers until they are at least two months old. Then they can eat kitten food. Do not give them dog food or food for adult cats. They are special. They need special food.

After every meal, carry them to the litter box. Gently set them down. They may not use it every time, but putting them in it after they eat will help them learn.

Keep water in one of its bowls. Rinse it out and add fresh water at least once a day. Don't let it get empty. Being a kitten is thirsty work.

Kittens need to eat three or four times a day. One idea is to buy samples or small cans of different food. This way they have choices. They may not like every food. However, if they don't eat or stop eating they may be sick. This is why going to a vet is so important.

Visiting the Vet

A few days after adopting your kitten, you will want to bring it to a veterinarian. This is a special doctor that only treats animals. Often rescue centers have their own veterinarians. If you adopted your kitten at a shelter or purchased it from a breeder, they will know a good vet. You can also ask friends with kittens.

The vet will give your kitten a check-up. He or she will tell you what shots your kitten will need. They will also be able to answer your questions.

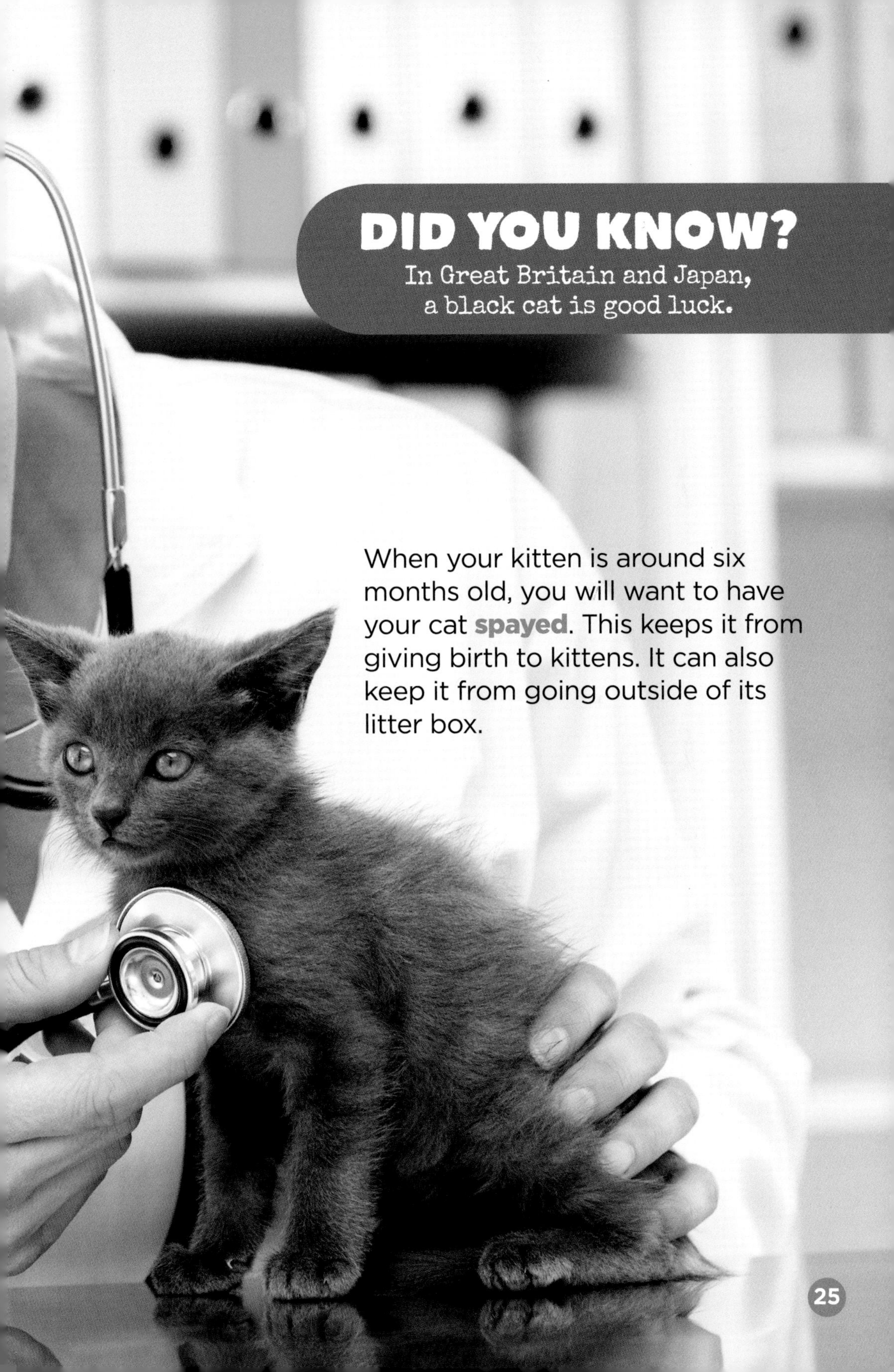

DID YOU KNOW?

In Great Britain and Japan, a black cat is good luck.

When your kitten is around six months old, you will want to have your cat **spayed**. This keeps it from giving birth to kittens. It can also keep it from going outside of its litter box.

Cat Safety

Walk around your neighborhood. You will probably see quite a few cats. Yet cats outside can have hard lives. They can be attacked by other animals. They can be hit by cars. Cats that stay indoors live longer.

Some people train their cats to walk using a leash. Start with a **harness**. Put it on your kitten at home. Later attach a leash or a lead. Let the kitten drag it around and get used to it. Then you can start walking it around your room. Use the leash when you take your cat outside.

Remember to keep windows shut in any room where the cat will be. Keep balcony doors closed as well.

Raising a happy kitty is hard work. Your kitten will pay it all back with love and purring.

SHOPPING LIST

When you are ready to bring home a kitten or a cat, have an adult take you to your local pet store. This is a list of some things you will need:

- ☐ Cat bed or box with warm blanket or towel
- ☐ Two Metal Bowls
- ☐ Cat Carrier
- ☐ Kitty Litter
- ☐ Litter Box
- ☐ Toys
- ☐ Premium Kitten Food
- ☐ Collar
- ☐ Leash or lead
- ☐ Brush
- ☐ Comb
- ☐ Safety cat collar with ID tag
- ☐ Scratching post or scratching pad

FIND OUT MORE

Online

There are a number of sites to learn about cat rescue centers in your area:

Alley cat rescue:
http://www.saveacat.org

Humane Society:
http://m.humanesociety.org

Petfinder:
https://www.petfinder.com/animal-shelters-and-rescues/search/

Several national pet supply chains have also partnered with rescue organizations. There are also "pet rescue days" held at fairs and swap meets.

Paws will help you get more involved with helping animals. They can also connect you with shelters:
https://www.paws.org/kids

Learn more about cats at:
http://kids.cfa.org

Pet names: Here's a fun site to find a great pet name.
https://www.bowwow.com.au

Here are tips for when you bring your new friend home:
https://www.petfinder.com/cats/bringing-a-cat-home/bringing-home-new-cat/

http://pets.webmd.com/cats/guide/newborn-kitten-care

http://www.vetstreet.com/our-pet-experts/your-guide-to-socializing-a-kitten

Books

Carney, Elizabeth. *Cats vs. Dogs*. Washington, DC: National Geographic Books, 2012.

Herlihy, Angela. *My First Cat Book: Simple and Fun Ways to Care for your Feline Friend*. New York: CICO Books, 2016.

Hutmacher, Kimberly M. *I Want a Cat*. Mankato, MN: Capstone, 2012.

Murray, Julie. *Kittens*. Edina, MN: ABDO, 2017.

Shojai, Amy. *Complete Kitten Care*. New York: New American Library, 2002.

Starke, Katherine. *Looking after cats and kittens*. UK: Usborne Publishing, Ltd., 2013.

GLOSSARY

adoption
Choosing or taking something as your own

breeding
The act of producing offspring

breeds
A particular type or kind of animal

carrier
Safe container to transport an animal

den
The resting place of animals

harness
Straps and fabric used to control an animal

independent
Free; thinking or acting for oneself

instincts
An inner force that causes an animal to act in a certain way

predators
An animal that hunts other animals for food

retractable
Able to be drawn back in

socialized
Comfortable playing and being around others

shelter
A place that provides food and protection for animals

spayed
To remove the organs that produce eggs from an animal

veterinarian
An animal doctor

BIBLIOGRAPHY

Canale, Larry. "Raining cat and dog facts: we've rounded up all kinds of interesting details about cats and dogs to bring you a little closer to your favorite pet." *Odyssey*, October 2013.

"Cats get jokes." *Muse*, September 2014.

"General Cat Care." The American Society for Prevention of Cruelty to Animals. https://www.aspca.org/pet-care/cat-care/general-cat-care.

Getschow, Kim. "The cat's meeeooow! (The Moscow Cats Theatre)." *Faces: People, Places, and Cultures.* Cobblestone Publishing Co., April 2011.

"Lucky or not?" *Cobblestone*, September 2016.

Sellers, Jennifer. "Entertainment for Cats: 5 Ways to Keep Kitty Happy." Petfinder. https://www.petfinder.com/cats/cat-care/entertainment-for-cats-5-ways-to-keep-kitty-happy/.

"10 Tips to Keep Your Cat Happy Indoors." Humane Society. http://m.humanesociety.org/animals/cats/tips/cat_happy_indoors.html.

INDEX

ABOUT THE AUTHOR

John Bankston

The author of more than 100 books for young readers, John Bankston lives in Miami Beach, Florida, with his ChiJack rescue dog named Astronaut. When he was a boy, he raised his cat George from a kitten.